Pound Puppies

Lovable, Huggable

The Puppy Who Couldn't Remember

by Johnson Hill
illustrated by Pat Paris

A GOLDEN BOOK • NEW YORK
Western Publishing Company, Inc., Racine, Wisconsin 53404

The trademark POUND PUPPIES and related character marks are used under license from Tonka Corporation. © 1986 Tonka Corporation. All rights reserved. Printed in the U.S.A. No part of this book may be reproduced or copied in any form without written permission from the publisher. GOLDEN®, GOLDEN & DESIGN®, and A GOLDEN BOOK® are trademarks of Western Publishing Company, Inc. Library of Congress Catalog Card Number: 85-81577. ISBN 0-307-16015-7/ISBN 0-307-66015-X (lib. bdg.)   A B C D E F G H I J

Early in the morning at the dog pound, the Pound
Puppies were sleeping soundly. Suddenly the gates opened
and Mr. Dabney Nabbit strode in, carrying his dogcatcher's
net over his shoulder. Something inside the net was
squirming and squeaking.

"Dag-nab-it! Wake up, you lazy mutts," Nabbit cried.
"Wait till you see what I scooped up this time!" And he set
down the net.

Out crept a little black-and-white spotted puppy. He looked around and began to cry.

The Nose was the first one to go up to the newcomer. "What's your name?" she asked. "Where do you come from?"

"I...I don't remember my name," whispered the puppy through his sobs. "I don't even remember where I live. All I know is that I have a home and friends and an important job."

"We'll help you," said The Nose. "And for now, we can just call you Pepper—because of your spots."

"OK," said the puppy, sniffing.

Soon it was breakfast time. All the Pound Puppies went to eat, and Pepper went with them.

"Hey, man, I'm Cooler," said the hound next to Pepper. He was the cool, calm leader of the Pound Puppies. "After we eat, you come with me. I'll take good care of you."

After breakfast Cooler took Pepper to see Doc Weston, the Pound vet.

"You're healthy," Doc said after examining Pepper. "But you have amnesia—you can't remember anything. You probably got hit on the head. My guess is that you'll get your memory back when you see, hear, or smell something familiar."

Fat tears rolled down Pepper's cheeks again.

"Hey, don't cry," said Cooler. "Come with me. I've got a treat for you."

Cooler led Pepper to the Pound Puppies' secret hideaway underneath the Pound.

"Nabbit doesn't know anything about this," said Cooler to Pepper as they entered a big room. It was furnished with sofas, TV's, a refrigerator, video games, and a ping-pong table.

"Oh, wow," said Pepper. "What a neat place."

After a snack of homemade dog biscuits, Pepper began to feel a little better.

"Now I'll introduce you to some of the others," Cooler said. He raised his voice and said, "Roll call!"

The Pound Puppies stopped what they were doing and snapped to attention in front of Cooler and Pepper.

"Scrounger!"

"Yes, boss," said Scrounger, the puppy who was good at finding things in garbage cans and dumps.

"Barkerville."

"Yes, sir," said a very elegant-looking puppy.

And Cooler went through all the rest of the line.

All the Pound Puppies except Cooler, Scrounger, Barkerville, and The Nose went back to what they had been doing, or off to do the chores Cooler assigned.

"Now for the next treat," Cooler said to Pepper. "We'll see if we can find your home."

"How will I know if it's my home if I can't remember anything?" asked Pepper.

"Don't forget what Doc said," Cooler reminded him. "You'll probably get your memory back when you see, hear, or smell something familiar."

Then the four Pound Puppies led Pepper to a hidden tunnel that went underneath the Pound wall. The tunnel's exit was through a fire hydrant that couldn't be seen from the Pound.

"You seem like the outdoor type," said The Nose. "How about if we start looking in the country?"

So the Pound Puppies and Pepper left the town behind them. They trotted up to a farmhouse. The farmer and his wife were sitting in rocking chairs on the porch.

"Why, look, Ma," said the farmer. "Here's a puppy. Cute little feller."

"Too bad we've already got a dog," said his wife.

The Pound Puppies looked out in the field. They saw a collie dog rounding up sheep.

As Pepper turned to go, he said, "I don't know how to round up sheep anyway. I'm sure I'm not a farm dog."

Near the town, the puppies came to a large white house with a big lawn. An elderly woman was sitting in front of the house in a large chair. On her lap was something shaggy that looked like a mop.

Suddenly the mop raised its head and yapped. It was a little Pekingese dog.

"Quiet, my dear Yum-Yum. Have these rude dogs upset you?" said the woman.

"Somehow I'm sure I'm not a lap dog," said Pepper as he and the Pound Puppies walked away.

Next the group came to a stand where newspapers were stored for delivery. There was a mutt trotting off with a rolled-up newspaper in his mouth. Other newspapers stuck out of the saddlebags on his back.

"That's a good outdoor job," said Pepper. "But somehow I'm sure I'm not a delivery dog. Oh, dear, oh, dear, what was my job?"

Finally the Pound Puppies visited the police station.

The police chief was just leaving the room. "Keep an eye on them, Laddy," he called over his shoulder. "I'll see if the cell is ready."

A German shepherd dog was guarding two prisoners.

"That doesn't look like fun," said Pepper. "I don't think I'm a guard dog either."

The puppies left the police station. They were ready to
give up for the day. Poor Pepper. Where was his home?
The Pound Puppies and Pepper started slowly back to the
Pound, their tails between their legs.

Suddenly Pepper stopped. He sniffed the air. His ears poked forward. His eyes lit up with excitement.

He smelled smoke.

"A fire!" he cried. "Follow me!"

The gang raced around the corner, with Pepper in the
lead. Ahead of them was a burning house. From inside the
house came cries for help.

"Wait here, fellows," said Pepper. "I know exactly what
to do."

He crawled into the house, and squirmed along the floor
where there was air to breathe. He found two children in
the living room and led them to safety.

Just then the Pound Puppies heard sirens. A big red fire truck pulled up to the burning house. Fire fighters jumped off the truck and hooked up their hoses to a fire hydrant. Pretty soon the fire was out.

Now the fire fighters ran to Pepper. "Where have you been, little pal? We've missed you. We've looked all over for you," they said.

At last Pepper had found his owners. And suddenly he remembered it all. He was a firehouse dog and his job was helping out at fires.

The Pound Puppies waved good-bye to Pepper.
"Good-bye, good-bye," they called. "Come and visit us
any time."